TRICERATOPS

The Horned Dinosaur

Benchmark Books
Marshall Cavendish Corporation
99 White Plains Road
Tarrytown, New York 10591-9001

Scientific consultant:
Rolf Johnson, Associate Curator of Paleontology;
Director, Science Media Center; Milwaukee Public Museum

Library of Congress Cataloging-in-Publication
Riehecky, Janet, date.
Triceratops: the [three-]horned dinosaur/ Janet Riehecky ;
illustrated by Susan Tolonen.
p.   cm -- (Dinosaur days)
Includes bibliographical references (p.   ) and index.
Summary: Describes a day in the life of the plant-eating triceratops, noting
its behavior, environment, and physical characteristics.
ISBN 0-7614-0602-6
1. Triceratops--Juvenile literature. [1. Triceratops. 2. Dinosaurs.]
I. Tolonen, Susan, date, ill. II. Title. III. Series: Riehecky, Janet, date. Dinosaur Days.
QE862.O65R55   1998   567.915'8--dc21   96-49421   CIP   AC

Printed in the United States of America

1 3 5 7 8 6 4 2

DINOSAUR DAYS

TRICERATOPS
The Horned Dinosaur

**WRITTEN BY JANET RIEHECKY
ILLUSTRATED BY SUSAN TOLONEN**

BENCHMARK BOOKS

MARSHALL CAVENDISH
NEW YORK

Triceratops bent her head. SNAP! She bit off a small branch from a bush. It tasted good. She slowly chewed the branch and its leaves. Then she reached for another. The front of her mouth was a sharp beak, like the beak of a bird. It made it easy for her to break off even very tough plants.

Every few bites, she glanced around. A young *Triceratops*, its horns not yet grown out, ate from a bush nearby. The leader of her herd, a male *Triceratops*, was also eating nearby. The herd was scattered throughout the area. Everything was just as it should be. *Triceratops* sniffed the air. No smell of danger. Good.

Triceratops
moved to a different
bush. The youngster
followed her. As *Triceratops*
tore a new branch from the bush,
she heard a bellow. She looked up.
Another male *Triceratops* stood near the
edge of the forest. He shook his horns and
bellowed again.

   Triceratops looked at the leader of her herd. So did
the new male. Then the new male walked slowly toward the leader. The
leader stood staring at him, shaking his horns back and forth. He had
been through this before. During most of the year, herd members lived
together peacefully. But sometimes, a young male *Triceratops* would
decide that he would like to be the leader of the herd. Then the males
fought to see who would be the leader. The leader had claimed this herd
by defeating another male, and he had fought before to keep it.

The herd leader stamped his feet and shook his horns again.
Sometimes he could frighten other males away just by showing
them how long his horns were. But this time, the other *Triceratops*
was not frightened. There was going to be a fight.

The two males began to circle each other. They shook their horns and stamped the ground. Suddenly, they attacked. The two dinosaurs charged at each other. CLASH! Their heads hit with a loud bang, and their horns locked together. The males pushed and twisted their heads back and forth, each trying to throw the other off balance.

9

The rest of the herd watched the fight. For a while, neither *Triceratops* was winning. Each pushed and twisted, trying to hit the side of the other with his horns, but neither one could. The horns struck only the bony frill that covered each dinosaur's neck and shoulders. Sometimes, in fights like these, a horn could puncture the frill. That might hurt one *Triceratops* badly enough that the other would win, but that didn't happen this time. The two dinosaurs fought on. Then, suddenly, the herd leader gave a fast twist and knocked the other off balance. Quickly, he thrust a horn into the other *Triceratops's* side.

It wasn't a bad wound, but it was enough. As blood dripped from his side, the other *Triceratops* broke away. He bowed his head, admitting he had lost, and stumbled away as quickly as he could. The herd leader let him go. The defeated *Triceratops* would rest for a while. Then he might try to fight a different herd leader—one he could beat.

After the fight, *Triceratops* returned to her meal. It didn't really matter to her who the leader of the herd was. She was more interested in filling her empty stomach.

Nearby, two young males, their horns barely grown out farther than their nose, decided it was time to play. They ran at each other, just as they had seen the older *Triceratops* do. Then they practiced pushing and twisting and turning to throw the other off balance. Sometimes a young *Triceratops* got hurt during one of these pretend fights, but not very often.

As *Triceratops* chewed on some leaves, she sniffed the air. Suddenly, the wind shifted. It brought a terrible smell her way. *Tyrannosaurus!* *Triceratops* didn't know its name, but she knew it was dangerous.

Before *Triceratops* could do anything, *Tyrannosaurus* rushed into the clearing. He headed for one of the young *Triceratops* that had been playing just moments before. *Triceratops* bellowed in alarm. Instantly, the herd reacted.

Tyrannosaurus could move quickly, but *Triceratops* was even faster. She chased the young *Triceratops* into the center of the clearing. The rest of the herd was gathering there.

If they had a choice, most *Triceratops* would run away from meat eaters. That was the safest thing to do. But when they couldn't run, they became fierce fighters. *Triceratops* steered the youngster behind the adults. Then she and the other adults formed a line in front of him.

Tyrannosaurus stomped toward them, roaring. Facing him was a row of *Triceratops*. *Triceratops* lowered her frill and swung her horns back and forth, threatening him. The other adults in her herd did the same.

Tyrannosaurus stopped and stared at them. Then he roared and lunged forward. He tried to bite *Triceratops*, but she moved too quickly. With a flip of her head, she sliced open *Tyrannosaurus's* leg with one horn. Roaring in anger, *Tyrannosaurus* retreated. He could find an easier meal somewhere else.

The *Triceratops* held their line until they were sure *Tyrannosaurus* was gone. Then they returned to their interrupted meals.

All too soon, the plants in the clearing were gone. The *Triceratops* ate everything within four or five feet (1.5 meters) of the ground, and so the herd needed to find another place to graze. As the days grew cooler, *Triceratops* and her herd moved south, eating as they traveled. Her herd joined with other small herds for the journey.

The *Triceratops* headed for the nesting
grounds they had used the year before. When
they reached their destination, *Triceratops* used
her feet, her beak, and her nose horn to hollow out
a large circle in the ground. She was making a nest
for her eggs. Any extra dirt that formed a mound
around the edge of the nest would help protect the eggs.

Other females worked nearby. Each nest was about
thirty feet (ten meters) from the next. This gave the
Triceratops room to walk between the nests without
stepping on any eggs.

When the nest was done, *Triceratops* laid her eggs. Then she gathered some leaves to cover the eggs. She wasn't trying to hide the eggs. The plants would help the eggs stay warm.

Triceratops and the other females watched their eggs after laying them. They chased away animals that tried to steal in and eat them. After the babies hatched, they would take care of the babies until they were big enough to take care of themselves.

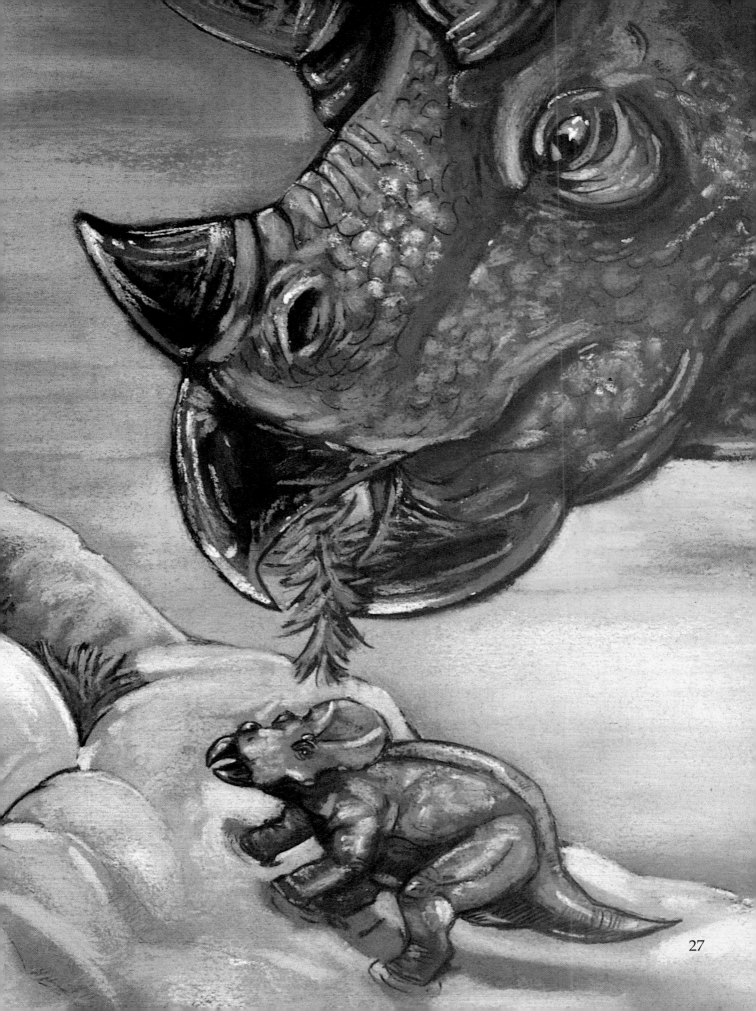

While *Triceratops* was waiting for the eggs to hatch, she didn't think much about her eggs. She did think about food. Soon she found a tasty bush and began munching.

SOME FACTS ABOUT . . . TRICERATOPS

Physical Appearance

Triceratops is one of the largest known horned dinosaurs. It could grow about thirty feet (nine meters) long and nine feet (three meters) high. It weighed about six tons (six tonnes).

The head of *Triceratops* was huge. On some skeletons, the skull took up almost one-third of the dinosaur's length. It grew three long, sharp horns on its head—one on its nose and one above each eye. The horn on its nose was short, but the ones over each eye could grow longer than three feet (one meter).

Triceratops also grew a large, bony frill, which covered its neck and shoulders. The frill may have worked like a shield to provide protection when the reptile fought an enemy or another *Triceratops*. *Triceratops* might also use its frill to show off. It could scare away some enemies or attract a mate by showing them how big its frill was. Some scientists think the frill also helped this dinosaur stay cool. An animal as large as *Triceratops* would have gotten very hot. As air passed over the frill, it could pull the heat out away from *Triceratops's* body.

Triceratops was a very strong dinosaur. It needed to be strong to hold up its large, heavy head and bulky body. It had big muscles and legs that were like stout pillars. There were four toes on each of its back legs and five on each front leg.

Scientists are not sure how the front legs of *Triceratops* fit together. Some think its legs sprawled to the side, the way crocodile legs do. Others think its legs were upright, like the legs of a rhinoceros.

Lifestyle

No one has ever seen a live *Triceratops*. The things *Triceratops* does in this book are just guesses about what it might have done. Scientists look for clues about how dinosaurs lived when they study the bones, claws, teeth, eggs, and footprints that dinosaurs left behind. Scientists also compare dinosaurs to animals that are alive today. For example, they study what animals with horns or antlers do today and imagine *Triceratops* doing the same things.

Triceratops's teeth tell us that it was a plant eater. It had a sharp beak at the front of its mouth that helped it break off tough plants. There were no teeth in the front of its mouth, but it had scissor-like teeth in its jaws. These teeth were very good at chopping up food. *Triceratops* probably spent much of its time just eating.

Scientists think that *Triceratops* could walk at a speed of about six miles (ten kilometers) an hour. They also think it could run as fast as fifteen miles (twenty-five kilometers) an hour if it had upright legs. If its front legs were sprawled, it could not have moved this quickly.

Scientists have not yet found any eggs of *Triceratops*. But they have found the eggs of other dinosaurs that lived in herds. Because these eggs were often broken at the top, with just a few cracks at the bottom, scientists have wondered whether the babies could take care of themselves soon after they hatched. If the babies had lived in the nests, with their mothers constantly taking care of them, it seems that they would have walked over the egg shells many times, crushing them into bits. The nests were built far enough apart, however, to give the mothers plenty of room to move around without stepping on the eggshells.

Scientists think that most horned dinosaurs, including *Triceratops*, lived in herds. They have found many sets of footprints of plant-eating dinosaurs traveling together. And in southern Alberta, Canada, they found a place containing the bones of a herd of about four hundred horned dinosaurs, called *Centrosaurus*.

GLOSSARY

bellow .... a loud, deep cry

frill .... a large bony plate that covered the neck and shoulders
of some dinosaurs

herd .... a large group of animals, all of one kind, that live
or travel together

nesting grounds ...... a large area of land where animals build nests for their eggs

retreat .... to leave a dangerous or difficult place

sprawled .... sticking out to the side

FOR FURTHER READING

Benton, Michael. *Dinosaurs: An A–Z Guide.* New York: Derrydale Books, 1988.

Dixon, Dougal. *The Big Book of Dinosaurs.* New York: Derrydale Books, 1989.

Johnson, Rolf E. and Carol Ann Piggins. *Dinosaur Hunt!* Milwaukee: Gareth Stevens Children's Books, 1992.

Lindsay, William. *American Museum of Natural History: Triceratops.* New York: Dorling Kindersley, 1993.

Lindsay, William. *The Great Dinosaur Atlas.* New York: Dorling Kindersley, 1991.

Norman, David. *The Illustrated Encyclopedia of Dinosaurs.* New York: Crescent Books, 1985.

Riehecky, Janet. *Triceratops.* Mankato, MN: The Child's World, 1988.

Sheehan, Angela. *Triceratops.* Windermere, FL: Ray Rourke Publishing Co., 1981.

Spanjian, Beth. *Baby Triceratops.* Chicago: Children's Press, 1988.

Stewart, Janet. *The Dinosaurs: A New Discovery.* Niagara Falls, NY: Hayes Publishing Co., 1989.

INDEX